The Possum
Always Rings Twice

Chet Gecko Mysteries

And don't miss

Chet Gecko's Detective Handbook (and Cookbook):
Tips for Private Eyes and Snack Food Lovers

A Politician in Peril . . .

Viola beckoned us closer.

"I'm running for student council president," she said. "And someone's trying to stop me."

The skinny sandpiper reached into a sweater pocket and handed me a much-folded paper.

I opened it. Crude block letters read:

U'LL NEVER BE PRESSIDNT IN A MILLYUN YEARS. GIVE UP NOW, OR U'LL BE IN RILLY BIG TRUBBLE.

"Now *that's* a threat," I said.

Viola took the note. "Track them down as soon as you can," she said. "The election is two days off."

"Fair enough," I said. "Now, there's just the small matter of our pay. We get fifty bucks a day."

The sandpiper squinched up her face. "I happen to know you get fifty *cents*," she said, "but I'll pay you seventy-five."

"Dang," I said to Natalie. "She's tough." I turned back to Viola. "Okay, we'll get right—"

But the sandpiper had slipped off.

"See that?" said Natalie. "She gets us all stirred up, promises us money, and then disappears."

"That's true."

"She'll make a great politician."

The Possum
Always Rings Twice

FROM THE TATTERED CASEBOOK OF

CHET GECKO
PRIVATE EYE

Bruce Hale

HARCOURT, INC.

Orlando • Austin • New York • San Diego • Toronto • London www.HarcourtBooks.com

First Harcourt paperback edition 2007

Excerpt from *Key Lardo* copyright © 2006 by Bruce Hale

The Library of Congress has cataloged the hardcover edition as follows:
Hale, Bruce.
The possum always rings twice/Bruce Hale.
p. cm.
Summary: Chet Gecko and his partner, Natalie Attired, try to find
out who is sending threatening notes to Viola Fuss, candidate
for student council president at Emerson Hicky Elementary School.
[1. Politics, Practical—Fiction. 2. Geckos—Fiction.
3. Animals—Fiction. 4. Schools—Fiction. 5. Humorous stories.
6. Mystery and detective stories.] I. Title.
PZ7.H1295Pos 2006
[Fic]—dc22 2005022197
ISBN 978-0-15-205075-7
ISBN 978-0-15-205233-1 pb

Text set in Bembo
Display type set in Elroy
Designed by April Ward

A C E G H F D B

Printed in the United States of America

To the cool Goff kids, Kellen and Jessie

The Possum
Always Rings Twice

A private message from the private eye ...

Down these mean streets a gecko must go. And as I've tramped along, I've picked up some hard-earned wisdom (along with the gum on my shoes). One thing I've learned: There's just not enough peace, love, and understanding in the world.

And that's a good thing. Otherwise, I'd be out of a job.

When life gets rough, tough, and tangled, that's where I come in. I'm Chet Gecko, Emerson Hicky Elementary's best lizard detective (and two-time dodgeball champ).

In my time, I've tackled cases stickier than a spider's handshake and harder than three-year-old boll weevil taffy. But nothing compares to the job that landed me knee-deep in school politics.

What seemed like a straightforward case of extortion took more twists and turns than an anaconda's lunch. It became a battle royal for control of the school. (Not that I necessarily believe school is worth fighting for, but a gecko's gotta do something with his days.)

While unraveling this sinister snarl, I also unearthed some ugly truths about politics. I discovered that politicians and diapers should both be changed regularly. (And for the same reason.)

And that in this country, anyone can grow up to become president. I guess it's just one of the risks we take.

In the end, my politicking landed me in one of the tightest spots I've ever encountered. Was I savvy enough to escape with my skin? Let me put it this way: Just like a politician, this is one private eye who always shoots from the lip.

1

The Boy Who Cried Wolverine

Let's face it: Elementary school is a jungle. Want to survive? Know your beasts. The herds of nerds, the packs of bullies, the rich kids, the jocks— each creature in this jungle has its own identifying marks.

Take Ben Dova, wolverine.

One look told the tale. Dagger claws, check. Furry boulders that passed for shoulders, check. B.O. strong enough to make a stinkbug cry, check.

Ben Dova might just as well have had *bully* stamped across his forehead.

He was big.

He was bad.

And he'd been hogging the tetherball for ten minutes.

Wolverine or no wolverine, I wanted to play.

"'Scuse me, bub," I said. "You almost finished?"

"Grrr," he replied.

Did I mention that Ben was also a brilliant conversationalist?

He planted a pair of hamlike fists on his hips, snorkeled some air through his nose, and scanned the scene.

"Pee-*yew*," he said. "What stinks?"

I gazed up at Ben. "Your armpits come to mind," I said. "As does your breath, your sister, and your grades. Pick one."

Ben's lip curled, flashing fangs that a great white shark would've envied.

I reached for the tetherball. "Hey, if you're not going to play . . ."

The wolverine hoisted the ball out of my reach. "Smells like barf," he said. "Smells like a pukey little lizard."

This brought some girlish giggles. A weasel and a rabbit stood nearby watching.

Sheesh. It's always worse with an audience.

My jaw tightened. "Look, pal. Why don't you give someone else a turn, and get back to practicing your tough-guy talk?"

Ben's bullet-hole eyes burned yellow. "You gonna make me, punk?"

Normally, I try to deal with bullies the Rodney Rodent way. (You know, the star of *Rodney Rodent's House of Cartoons*?) Rodney always says: Don't show fear; speak firmly but politely; and just walk away.

I didn't show fear. Speaking firmly, I said, "I don't make beanheads, I bake them."

I've always had problems with the polite part.

Turning to go, I nodded to the girls. A paw like a catcher's mitt swung at my head.

I ducked.

The gleam in Ben's eyes went from yellow to red. That was my cue.

"Yaaah!"

I pelted across the blacktop, straight for the nearest portable classroom. Mere steps ahead of the wolverine, I reached it.

Fa-zzup! I scuttled up the wall.

Whether you're a PI like me or just a fourth grader trapped in a sixth-grade world, it pays to have serious climbing skills. In three shakes, I made the roof.

"Come back here, Gecko!" yelled Ben Dova.

I laughed. "If you think I'm coming down to get creamed, you're so dumb you put lipstick on your forehead to make up your mind."

A snarl below told me the joke had found its mark. I savored the moment.

"Verrry funny," came an oily voice from behind me. "You should try stand-up."

A huge brown bat hovered in midair.

"I did," I said, "but I kept falling down."

"Too bad you didn't fall farther," she crooned.

Swell. Another bully. Even for Emerson Hicky, this was excessive.

"What is this, Let's Pick on a PI Week?"

The bat wore a dorky pink hair ribbon and a savage sneer. Her smooshed-in nostrils twitched as if she smelled something stenchy.

As if that something was me.

She opened her mouth to speak.

I held up a hand. "I know, I know," I said. "I'm a smelly little lizard and blah-blah-blah."

"Verrry perceptive," said the bat.

"Look, Flappy, can we just skip to the part where I run away? It takes me a while to come up with new insults."

The bat smiled, baring fangs as yellow as a stale harvest moon.

"But of course," she said. Miss Flappy flexed her wings.

I sprinted for the nearest treetop.

Flump-flump-flump! The thrumming of bat wings grew louder.

My leafy sanctuary was only steps away.

Some instinct said *duck!* The bat's swoop trickled chills down my spine.

I stumbled headlong—off the roof and into a tree.

"*Unh—*

      Ooh—

            Ach!"

Plummeting downward, I bounced from limb to limb like a deranged pinball. Finally I landed— *ka-whump!*—in a heap on the grass.

Dizzier than a carload of cheerleaders, I struggled to my knees. Then a large brown shape landed nearby. A massive black-and-tan figure rounded the corner.

Bullies to the left, bullies to the right.

I was doomed.

2

Every Frog Has His Day

As I was composing my will, something that looked like a cactus on steroids strolled up between Miss Flappy and Ben Dova.

My rescuer?

"Well, well, a stinkin' gecko."

Nope. It was Rocky Rhode, horned toad—torturer, shakedown artist, and tiddlywinks champion.

Yet *another* bully. Was I a magnet for morons?

But her next words surprised me.

"See, what did I tell you?" she said to the other thugs. Rocky grabbed their shoulders. "Three of us tackling one chump, while out there"—she indicated the playground—"all those suckers are going to waste."

Ben growled. "No horny toad can be the boss of me."

"I don't wanna be," she said. "Just listen." Rocky smoothly turned the bullies and led them away.

"But," said Miss Flappy, glancing back at me, "he's—"

"That yo-yo?" said Rocky. "Relax. He's not going anywhere."

And just like that, they walked off.

My jaw dropped. What was *that* all about?

"Looks like you're too boring for the bullies," someone chirped.

A spiffy-looking mockingbird perched on a limb of the tree, grooming her feathers. It was my partner, Natalie Attired. A true friend, she put the *wise* in wisecrack and the *dis* in disrespectful.

Natalie had my back, and I had hers. Which reminded me . . .

"Hey, I thought you were my partner," I said.

"Last time I checked," said Natalie.

I got to my feet and retrieved my hat. "So where were you when those mugs were getting ready to clean my clock?"

"Just where you always said I should be: on the lookout."

"And what were you looking at?"

She glided down to the lawn. "You, about to get pounded."

I shook my head, temporarily speechless.

"I know," said Natalie. "I'm amazing. You don't deserve a partner like me."

"Birdie," I said, "you took the words right out of my mouth."

Don't get me wrong. A detective's life isn't always this chock-full of danger, chills, and near disaster.

Sometimes it's worse.

Still, the next hour or so passed pleasantly enough. (If you don't count the horrors of history class. Learning about the long-ago doings of dead people always gives me the willies.)

Then came lunch—the only subject I always ace. The lunch ladies were dishing up blowfly burritos with grasshopper guacamole and mantis-meal cakes.

Gotta love that south-of-the-border cuisine.

After scarfing a second helping (thanks to my cafeteria contacts), I leaned back on the bench and patted my gut. Nothing beats a full belly.

Even Natalie's lame jokes couldn't spoil my mood.

"Hey, Chet," she said as we left the lunchroom, "here's one you should know. What do you call cheese that doesn't belong to you?"

"I don't know, and I don't care."

"Nacho cheese!" Natalie cackled.

I groaned.

Natalie and I ambled toward the playground and scoped out the scene. Two ferrets stuffed a toad in a trash can. A marmot spray-painted graffiti on the gym wall. And a bunch of sixth graders used a first grader as a volleyball.

Some say a little knowledge is a dangerous thing. But sometimes, just showing up for school is what's hazardous.

We were strolling past a soccer game, when—
Bim-bam-boomf!

A blurry yellow-green ball bounced out of nowhere, straight into my gut.

"Oog!" I staggered back, feeling my burritos rearrange themselves.

"Hi, hi, hi!" said the ball. It was Popper, a hyperactive tree frog with all the charm and tact of a runaway chain saw.

We had once befriended her on a case. We were still paying for that mistake.

The third grader hopped around us. "I'm glad, so glad, I bumped into you."

"That makes *one* of us," I said, rubbing my belly.

"You guys gotta help, hippety-help me," Popper squeaked.

"No problem, short stuff," I said, pointing. "The loony bin is *that* way."

Natalie elbowed me. "What's up, Popper?"

The frog looked from one of us to the other with

eyes big as punch bowls. "Could you please, pretty please, sign my petition?" She thrust a paper at us.

I glanced at it. "*You're* running for student council president?"

"Yup, yep, uh-huh."

"Been collecting signatures long?"

Popper's head bounced up and down like a BB on a bongo drum. "One, two, three-three days!"

"But there are no names," said Natalie.

The tree frog shrugged. "My mommity-mom said student council would be a good way to make friends."

Natalie and I exchanged a glance.

"We'll sign it," I said. "But don't get any ideas."

"Thank you, thank you," said Popper. "You guys are the best!"

I couldn't argue with her about that. We scrawled our names, and Popper bounced off to torment someone else.

"What a weird day," I said. "Bullies get bored, and Popper runs for president. What's next?"

"You, actually doing some homework?" said Natalie.

"Don't make me laugh, birdie."

But the answer wasn't long in coming. And when it came, it brought more trouble than a busload of candy-crazed chipmunks on Halloween night.

3

Too Marvelous for Birds

Natalie and I had just settled under the scrofulous tree to hash over our last case. I fished a package of Cheese Nits from my pocket. (No reason lunch should interfere with my snacking schedule.)

Leaves crunched behind the tree. A bird's beak poked around it.

"Er, tell me, are you Chet Gecko?" asked the bird in a nasal voice.

"If we can believe what his mom says," Natalie chirped.

I glared. "I've told you before: Lay off my mama."

The bird cleared her throat. "Er, Chet Gecko, the detective?"

"No," I said, crunching a couple of Cheese Nits,

"Chet Gecko, the brain surgeon. We're offering free lobotomies today. Want one?"

The bird frowned. My wit has that effect on some folks.

"Relax," said Natalie. "He won't bite—unless you're a burrito."

"Very well," said the bird.

At that, a skinny sandpiper followed her long beak into view. Her licorice jujube eyes jittered from side to side, alert for trouble. A faded lemon

yellow sweater draped her compact body, and she teetered on legs like a couple of bent shish-kebab skewers.

"Viola Fuss," she said with a nervous nod.

"I don't know," I said, "vhy?"

If birds had lips, hers would've compressed into a thin line. "Very funny. They said you were prone to mirth."

"Remind me to thank them. Who are you?"

"Viola Fuss," said the sandpiper again. "That's my name."

"That's too bad," said Natalie.

"Er, I want to hire you."

Natalie's eyes found mine. A fresh case!

I jumped up. "Why didn't you say so? Sit down and take a load off, sister."

A twig fell from the tree, and Viola skittered away at the sound.

"Too much espresso in your eggnog?" asked Natalie.

The sandpiper retreated behind the tree. "Can we get out of the open?"

"Why?" I asked.

"I don't want anyone to see me."

I planted my hands on my hips. "Oh, so we're okay to hire, but we're too low-class to be seen with?"

Viola scanned the scene from her hiding place. "No, that's not it—although I confess your reputation is spotted at best..."

"You should see his T-shirts," said Natalie.

The sandpiper beckoned us closer. We moved in.

"I'm afraid if I'm seen with you, whoever's threatening me might learn that I've hired a detective. And if that happens, things could get ugly."

"Whoa there, cowgirl," I said. "Back up your pony. Why are you being threatened? Have you been picking your toes in Pottawatomie?"

"Blowing bubbles without using your mouth?" asked Natalie.

The sandpiper did that disapproving thing with her beak again. "I'll have you know I'm running for student council president," she said. "And someone's trying to stop me."

"Are you sure?" I asked.

"Positive," said Viola. "Already I've received two notes in my locker."

"What's your locker number?" asked Natalie.

"Two thirty-three," said Viola. "Why?"

"Why not?" I said. "Go on."

She blinked. "Anyway, the first note said, er, *You can't win; drop out now.*"

I smirked. "Some threat. Sure it's not about the spelling bee?"

The skinny bird reached into a sweater pocket and handed me a much-folded paper. "I think not," she said. "Here's the second note."

I opened it. Crude block letters read:

I'M NOTT KIDDING. U'LL NEVER BE
PRESSIDNT IN A MILLYUN YEARS.
GIVE UP NOW, OR U'LL BE IN RILLY
BIG TRUBBLE.

"Now, *that's* more like a threat," I said, feeling a thrill of the old excitement.

"Well, we know one thing," said Natalie.

"What's that?"

"Whoever wrote it definitely isn't in the spelling bee."

Viola took the note. "Track them down as soon as you can," she said. "Then, report them to Principal Zero. The election is just two days off."

"Fair enough," I said. "Now, there's just the small matter of our pay. We get fifty bucks a day, plus expenses."

The sandpiper squinched up her face. "I happen to know you get fifty *cents,*" she said, "but I'll pay you seventy-five."

"Dang," I said to Natalie. "She's tough." I turned back to Viola. "Okay, we'll get right—"

But the sandpiper had slipped off through the trees.

"See that?" said Natalie. "She gets us all stirred up, promises us money, and then disappears."

"That's true."

"She'll make a great politician."

4

Full Speech Ahead!

How do you dig up suspects? Well, you could go down to Crazy Jimmy's Creeps 'n' Cranks and pick a few off the rack. But you usually get the best results by asking one simple question: Who benefits?

At least that's what Natalie said as we headed off.

"Who benefits from Viola dropping out?" I echoed. "Well . . . the other candidates, for one . . ."

"Her enemies, for another . . . ," Natalie said.

"Um . . . her ballet teacher?"

"Ballet teacher? Why?"

I scratched my chin. "Because . . . if she's not on student council, she'll have more time to run around in a tutu?"

Natalie raised an eyebrow.

"Hey, I'm brainstorming here," I said.

"For now, let's stick to the other candidates," she said.

"Like superglue shorts."

Just then, we were passing the gym. Natalie gawked at a fancy purple poster announcing a lunchtime speech by Perry Winkel, presidential candidate.

"I believe that's what we in the detective biz call a lead," I said.

"Ah, my wisdom is rubbing off on you."

"As long as that's all that rubs off, birdie."

We made for the rally. I noticed the graffiti on the gym wall had spread. FUR IS FIRST! and DOWN WITH FEATHERS! had joined other popular slogans like KYLE RULEZ, JOANIE LUVS CHA-CHA, and 2GOOD + 2B = 4BIDDEN.

And they say kids don't like to write.

Rounding the corner of the building, we ran smack into a good-sized crowd blocking the hall-way.

"Hey, watch it!" said the rat I'd bumped.

"Is this all for Perry's speech?" asked Natalie.

The rat ignored her, so I scaled a pole for a better view.

My perch revealed the tops of a lot of kids' heads, and beyond them, a kit fox standing tall on a stage set against the gym's outside wall. Behind him hung a banner: PERRY 4 PREZ! As he raised his paws, the hubbub quieted.

"Friends," said the fox, "I'm here to tell y'all that the trouble's getting troublin' at Emerson Hicky. We're headed for big-time danger."

"I've been saying that for years," I said.

"Shh!" hissed the rat below me.

The fox I took to be Perry Winkel furrowed his brow. "We have friends and we have anemones. And now, some low-down critters wants to undermine everythin' we stand for."

"Moles?" asked a plump pigeon.

"No, not moles," he said. "Baddies. Terriers who hold our school hostile. They're tryin' to destroy our very Emerson Hicky-ness."

"Don't let 'em!" someone shouted.

"I will force these fightses of darkness," said Perry. "I will sit in that presidental chair, standin' tall. Together, I will make this school the kinda place you'll be proud as punch to attend."

"He says he's gonna give everyone punch," I told Natalie.

"No cookies?" she asked.

"SHH!" said the rat again.

A newt raised his hand. "Hey, who are these baddies and terriers?" he said.

"Don't bother your noggin," said Perry Winkel. "I stand for things. So vote for me, and remember: A burn in the hand is worth two in the bush!"

He flashed a smile and raised his arms in a V for victory.

The group cheered. "Perry for *Prez*! Perry for *Prez*!" they chanted. Three weasels started passing out free bubble gum.

Say what you will about the speech, this guy knew his voters.

I slid down the pole and joined Natalie.

"Let's interview him," she shouted over the din.

"Great idea," I yelled back, snagging some gum.

Then a ripple swept the crowd, bringing silence in its wake. Kids cleared back as if you could catch ten pages of math homework just by breathing the air.

Past a couple of cringing gophers, I saw the problem: a line of bullies, shoulder to shoulder, tromping down the corridor.

Among them swaggered Erik Nidd, Herman the Gila Monster, Ben Dova, Miss Flappy, Bosco Rebbizi, and smack-dab in the middle, Rocky Rhode. They marched with a menace designed to intimidate.

It worked.

My tail twisted. What serious mischief were they up to?

Kids jumped back into the shrubbery or flattened themselves against the wall to avoid the bully juggernaut. Rocky sneered left and right with satisfaction.

"Boo!" said Erik to a second-grade shrew. She fainted dead away.

"That's what I'm speechin' about," shouted Perry Winkel, safe on the sidelines behind his supporters. "The dangers of the school is dangerous—*augh!*"

He shrieked in fear as Herman glared at him.

"Herman says zip it, fox," the Gila monster growled.

The fox zipped it.

The line of thugs rolled on, smooth and steady as the *Titanic* on Rollerblades (and just as full of potential disaster). Strangely enough, they didn't break ranks. Stranger still, they didn't break any heads. They just kept tramping.

"Eerie, isn't it?" said Natalie.

"Eerie doesn't begin to cover it," I muttered.

As the marchers drew even with us, Ben Dova swiveled his head and locked eyes with me. His stare could've fried eggs in a blizzard.

But the tough-guy effect was ruined when he stumbled into Herman.

"Watch it," rumbled the Gila monster.

"*You* watch it," said Ben.

"Clumsy."

"Cheesehead."

"Dorkus."

Rocky Rhode broke ranks and slipped between them. "Guys, guys," she said. "Try to get along just this once. Trust me—if we all pull together..."

The rest of her comment was lost in a whisper. The band of bullies swept on down the hall. Around us, half a hundred kids let out their breath.

"That whole thing was fishier than the bottom of a pelican's lunch box," I said.

"What do you suppose it was all about?" asked Natalie.

But before we could speculate, the class bell jangled, leaving us with a bad case of *mysteriosus interruptus*. I wanted to keep investigating, but school waits for no gecko.

Not even if he begs.

5

Throw Your Brat into the Ring

Afternoon recess couldn't come soon enough to suit me. (Of course, that's usually the case.) When the bell rang, I shot from my seat like a loogey from an anteater's tongue.

Natalie met me at the playground's edge. "So what's the plan, Stan?" she asked. "Check out the bully boys?"

"Naw. Let's grill Perry Winkel and Viola's other rivals. Then we'll see if the Thug Parade connects with our case."

"Take it away, Trey," she said.

I gave her a look. "Just cool it with the rhyming names, okay?"

"You bet, Chet."

We struck out, keeping an eye peeled for the kit fox. A commotion drew us toward the jungle gym. But something brought us up short.

That something was a small green-and-yellow shape. It soared over the heads of the small crowd, bounced a couple of times, and landed at our feet.

"Hey, hi, ho," Popper the tree frog croaked weakly.

"Making new friends on the campaign trail?" I asked.

The little amphibian shook her head. "I already got all my siggy-saggy signatures," she said. "I just wanted to play. But those biggity-bad bullies kicked me out."

Natalie helped Popper rise. "Why did they pick on you?"

"No idea," said the frog. "Beats mu-mi-mo-me."

I glanced at Natalie. We knew that Popper could annoy people in her sleep from a distance of twelve miles without even breaking a sweat.

"Really, really, and truly," said Popper. "They said, no frogs allowed, then they gave me the heave-ho-ho-ho."

"We should do something," Natalie said to me.

I looked at the knot of kids by the jungle gym—all ferrets, weasels, and badgers, all bigger than me.

"You're right," I said. "We should mind our own beeswax. Popper, tell me: How do you feel about the other candidates, like Viola Fuss?"

The tree frog frowned in confusion. "Um, they're okely-dokely-doo," she said. "Always been friendly to me. Why?"

"No reason, squirt," I said. "Stay away from those bullies, now."

The tree frog hopped slowly off. Natalie and I gave the jungle gym a wide berth, and the punks gave us the traditional punk salute. (It involved sneers, jeers, and multiple hand gestures.)

"Okay," I said. "Scratch one suspect."

"We could've done that before you talked to her," said Natalie. "I can't imagine Popper writing a threatening note."

I smiled. "Except for one saying she'd like a play-date. That's pretty threatening."

We tracked down Perry Winkel by the swings. He and a slinky mink were buttonholing some kids as we approached.

"...hope we can count on you to count your vote," the fox was saying.

"Yeah, definitely!" said one of the students, a cheery rabbit.

Natalie and I stopped beside them. "Hey, Perry," I said. "How's about we ask you a few questions?"

He eyed me dubiously. The mink said, "Do you mind?"

"No, I don't mind asking questions," I said. "It's my job."

I gave her the once-over. She was a long, tall drink of chocolate milk. Her eyes glittered like the prize in a Cracker Jack box, and she was wrapped from head to toe in the finest fur. (Of course, you'd expect that in a mink.)

"I meant, do you mind waiting?" purred the mink, in a voice like butterscotch pudding over steel. "We're busy."

I turned to the rabbit and his pals. "Look, Flopsy," I said. "Why don't you and your friends hop on down the bunny trail? We want a private chat."

"Yeah, definitely!" said the rabbit. He and his buddies bounced off.

"Now you're not busy," said Natalie.

The mink swished her long tail. "I'm not sure I like you interfering in our campaign," she said.

"I'm not sure I like twenty-page tests and surly teachers," I said. "But they keep on coming. I'm Chet Gecko, PI. This is my partner, Natalie."

"I'm Nadia Nyce," said the mink.

"Of course you are," I said.

"What's the subject of yer speakin', friend?" asked Perry Winkel.

"Oh, just a little skullduggery," I said. "Been getting any threatening notes?"

The kit fox's pointed kisser wore a frown. "Me, personably? No . . ."

"Been writing any?" asked Natalie.

"Of course not!" said Nadia, cutting in. "That's outrageous!"

I crossed my arms. "Is it?" I asked. "Someone's been trying to scare Viola Fuss into quitting the race."

"Why point the finger of fate at me?" said Perry. "I'm just a babe in the wolves." His furry face was as blank as a blackboard in the summertime.

The kit fox was either dumb as a stump or a very good liar, or, well, both.

Natalie spread a wing. "What better suspect than Viola's main rival?"

The mink scoffed. "But why Perry?" she said. "It could just as easily have been another candidate. Popper, for instance."

"Nah," said Natalie and I together.

"Okay, then. What about Ben Dova?"

"What about him?" I said. "He's a mook."

"He's a candidate," said Perry. "Why aren't y'all givin' *him* the thirty-third degree?"

I exchanged a puzzled glance with Natalie.

"That lug, a candidate?" I asked. "Is he running on the Bully Ticket?"

"Why don't you ask him?" said the mink, smoothing her fur. "And by the way, how do you know Viola's threats are real?"

I frowned. "What do you mean?"

The mink leaned in. "I heard that the pressure is getting to her, that Viola had a nervous breakdown. Maybe she's imagining things."

"Wha-at?"

"That's silly," said Natalie. "We saw the note."

"Did you?" said Nadia. "Or did she write it herself in a desperate bid for sympathy and votes?" She took Perry's arm and started off. "I'd get your facts straight before you accuse innocent students."

"And then, I'd cast y'all's vote for myself," called Perry Winkel. "The election's three days after yesterday!"

Natalie and I watched them go, then we headed back across the grass.

"What do you make of them?" I said.

"A double twosome of two-ness," said Natalie in a spot-on imitation of Perry's twang. "His sentences sound like they've been through a blender."

"And I'm not sure whether Nadia's giving us straight talk or hot air."

"Well, there's one way to find out," said Natalie, raising her eyebrows.

"Let her blow up a balloon?"

"Stake out Viola's locker and see who shows up."

"Birdie," I said, "sometimes you say the smartest things."

Natalie ducked her head. "Gee, thanks, Chet."

"Sometimes, but not often."

6

The Fountain of Brutes

Recess was disappearing like the last sips of a malted earwig milk shake. Time was short. But we had saved just enough of it for a quick stakeout.

Natalie and I hustled down the hall to the lockers. With luck, we might catch some creepo in the act and answer two questions: Who was behind the threats, and was our client loonier than a dodo bird in a disco contest?

We loitered by the drinking fountain near Viola's locker. All seemed normal. Students flowed up and down the hall, retrieving books, chatting with friends, and savoring their last minutes of freedom.

Twice, we thought we spotted kids trying to slip something into her locker, but it turned out to be

neighbors stowing things in their own. Still, we waited.

Detective work makes me thirsty. I turned to the drinking fountain, and put my hand on the lever.

"Don't look now," said Natalie, "but we may have a live one."

While bending to drink, I casually glanced to the side.

A sneaky-looking weasel in a fluorescent orange tank top lingered by Viola's locker, fumbling in a book bag. Was this our suspect?

Keeping an eye on her, I pressed the lever again and lowered my mouth to sip cool water.

Instead, I sucked up a mouthful of hair.

"Bleah!"

I spit out the fur and swiveled my head. A thick paw blocked the fountain.

"Do you mind, fuzzy?" I said. "I'm trying to drink."

"Not here, you're not," a voice rumbled.

Straightening, I found myself eye-to-belly with a gray shag rug. I looked up, up, up and spotted a fat head at the top of it. A badger with a face like a frying pan stared down at me. His eyes were deader than a zombie's houseplants.

"It talks," I said.

"Actually, it doesn't," said Natalie. "The one behind it did the talking."

A familiar face leered over the badger's shoulder. Ben Dova, wild wolverine and prime suspect.

"Just the political animal I wanted to see," I said.

"Nuts to you," said Ben.

The badger scowled. "This ain't your water fountain," he squeaked, in a voice like a duck on helium. "Beat it, Gecko."

I eased back out of reach. "Not without some answers. Tell me, Ben, do you threaten all the candidates, or just Viola?"

"You don't listen so good," said Ben. "Lousy lizards can't drink here. Ain't that right, Dum-Dum?"

"*You* catch on quick, pal," said the badger.

A semicircle of kids had formed at a safe distance, glad to witness someone else's troubles. No one stepped forward to help.

"And a body can't walk around without a brain," I said, "but here you are. Anyway, the drinking fountains are for everyone."

The wolverine's growl rumbled like evil dwarfs bowling underground.

"Not no more," said Dum-Dum. "Can't you read?"

I looked where his long claw pointed. On the wall above the spigot, a hand-lettered sign read, MAMMULS OLNY!!!

What the heck?

"You can't do that," said Natalie. "It's not right."

"It's right if we say it's right," said Ben.

"I don't mean *fair* right; I mean *right* right," said my partner. "Right?"

"Right," I said.

"Huh?" said the wolverine.

"It's misspelled," said Natalie. "*Only* is o-n-l—"

"Shaddap!" snarled Dum-Dum. "Ben, we gotta teach these punks a lesson."

"If it's an English lesson," I said, "don't bother."

Natalie and I backed away. The two bruisers advanced on us like a pair of tanks against tricycles.

This was going to get very ugly. Very quickly.

"C'mere, Gecko," said the wolverine. "Time to take your medicine."

I sidestepped his grab. "Not unless it's sugar-coated."

The badger reached for Natalie, who took flight. He snagged her leg.

"Chet!" cried Natalie.

"Let her go!" I shouted.

"What's going on?" A buzz-saw voice sliced through the hubbub.

Kids parted, and up waddled an alligator in a pill-box hat. She was mean, she was green, but I'd never been happier to see the Detention Queen—Ms. Glick, the Beast of Room 3.

"Ms. Glick," I said. "Natalie and I—"

The Beast of Room 3 whirled on me. "Chester Gecko!"

I hate it when they call me by my full name.

"Making trouble?" she said. "What a surprise."

"Not me," I said. "These punks were just about to—"

Her eyes narrowed. "Don't try to pass the buck. Detention for you tomorrow, mister."

"But—"

"Mr. Dumbrowski!" said the alligator, turning to Dum-Dum.

"Um, yeah?" squeaked the badger.

"Put down that mockingbird right now. Everyone, back to class."

B-r-r-ring!

The bell rang, underlining her words. I sighed.

It wasn't fair; it wasn't pretty. But what's a gradeschool detective to do? The teachers hold all the cards, and it's a stacked deck anyway.

Off to class I went.

7

The Squirrelly Bird Gets the Squirm

The next day dawned hot and sunny as a super-model's smile. At least, that's what Natalie told me.

I missed the dawn, missed my alarm clock, and, what's worse, even missed breakfast.

Mornings are not my best time of day.

Ten minutes before the school bell, I straggled onto campus and met Natalie by the flagpole. The hind end of a worm was vanishing into her mouth as I approached. (Or maybe it was the front end; with worms it's hard to tell.)

"Hey, *mmf,* sleepyhead!" she mumbled around the worm. "You're the late bird, so you don't get one of these."

"I'll try to live with the disappointment," I said. "Shall we snoop?"

As Natalie and I headed back to Viola's locker to resume our stakeout, we chewed over the case. It wasn't as tasty as breakfast would have been.

"So, who's left on our suspect list?" I said.

"Perry Winkel and Ben Dova," said Natalie. "My money's on Perry."

"But he's the front-runner," I said. "Why would he threaten Viola?"

Natalie shrugged. "He's gone nutso for power?"

"A cuckoo fox? Maybe. But I'm betting that Ben's our boy."

We passed the office. Down the hall, our sandpiper client was doing some early morning politicking, talking to passersby.

"... hope I can count on your vote," she was saying to a nerdy chipmunk.

"Sure," he said, "if you'll really consider my idea of putting cola in the drinking fountains. It's highly feasible."

Viola passed the little rodent a slip of cardboard that read, *Vote for Viola!*

The chipmunk looked at it. "Perry's giving out *gum,*" he sneered, and left.

"Hey, Viola," I said.

She gave a start and scuttled away. "Oh!" she said. "It's you."

"We just wanted to ask—" Natalie began.

"Don't look at me!" squeaked Viola. "Eyes

front!" She scampered behind a shaggy skreezitz bush.

Natalie raised an eyebrow. We pretended to gaze across the schoolyard.

"Ooo-kay," I said. "Happy?"

"You know I'm not happy," said Viola. "Someone's spreading rumors that I've had a, er, nervous breakdown."

"The nerve of them," said Natalie.

"And today I found another threatening note."

I turned. "What's it say?"

"Don't look!" shrieked the sandpiper.

After I faced front, she tossed a piece of paper onto the ground at our feet. The note read:

THIS IS YER LAST CHANCE. QUITT
BY LUNCHTYME, OR YER TOAST!

Mmm, toast. That reminded me: I hadn't eaten yet.

"Chet?" said Natalie.

"Hmm?"

"What do you think?"

"I think a Termite Twinkie would help me make it to lunchtime."

Natalie swatted me. "About the note, ding-dong."

"Oh, right."

The bushes rustled. "Can you, er, stop this lunatic?" asked Viola.

"Definitely," I said.

"Soon?" she asked. "I'm giving a speech at recess, and I'm afraid."

"Buck up, sister. Tell me: Aside from the other candidates, has anyone got it in for you?"

"Impossible," said Viola, poking her head through the bush. "I'm a straight-A student, president of four clubs, captain of the girls' soccer team, editor of the school newspaper, and first-chair tuba."

"And who could carry a grudge against such perfection?" I said.

"Nobody," said the sandpiper. "Just ask the librarian."

"Cool Beans?" said Natalie. "Why?"

"He's running the election. All the candidates have to—"

A cheerleader approached.

"*Shh!*" hissed the sandpiper. "Act naturally."

I studied a cloud as if it contained the secrets of turning water into chocolate syrup. Natalie began to whistle "Boogie Wonderland."

The cheerleader passed us. "You guys are so weird," she said.

I turned to Natalie. "Then I guess we were acting naturally," I said. "Good enough for you, Viola?"

No reply.

"Viola?"

But when we searched the bush, our client had skedaddled.

"Where'd she go?" asked Natalie.

"Beats me," I said. "But I know where *I'm* going."

"Where?"

"To see about that Termite Twinkie."

Staking out Viola's locker seemed a waste of time, since she had already received another note (or made one up—I wasn't ruling out her nuttiness).

Natalie split for class. I hit the snack zone.

For a handful of quarters, the vending machine coughed up its treasure of termitey goodness. I had just peeled the wrapper and chomped into the treat, when the unmistakable sound of tough-guy patter reached my ears.

"Hold it right there, Gecko."

I looked up. My path was blocked by two rats wearing shades. One was short and burly, the other tall and gangly.

"I'm already holding it," I said. "Mind if I keep on eating it?"

Short-and-Burly snarled, "That ain't all you'll be eatin' if you don't listen up."

"Be still, my beating heart. Is that a threat?"

Tall-and-Gangly cracked her knuckles.

Burly sneered. "Look, peeper, I'm only gonna tell you once."

"Good," I said. "Then I'll only be half as bored."

Burly snapped his fingers. Gangly lifted me by my shirtfront, leaving my feet dangling.

"Stay away from Ben Dova," said the shorter rat.

"I'm trying," I said. "He won't let me."

"Try harder," said Burly.

"Is that all?" I asked Gangly. She gave me the stone face.

"Nah," said Burly. "If I even hear Chet Gecko and Ben Dova mentioned in the same sentence, your bum is gum, and I'm the chewer."

"Does that last sentence count?" I asked Gangly. Still no response.

Burly smiled. "Nah," he said. "I'm givin' you one for free."

I smiled back. "Since you're so generous, I don't suppose you'll confess who told you to lean on me?"

"You don't suppose right," he said.

"Okay, then, tell me something." I pointed at Gangly. "She never cracks a smile. Why do you have her along?"

The short rat looked up at the taller one. "For her fine conversation," he said.

Burly snapped his fingers again. Gangly hoisted me overhead, bent her knees, and lofted me into the trash can. A picture-perfect hook shot.

"Plus she's one heckuva ballplayer," said Burly. "The girl got game."

Wriggling upright in the can, I watched the cut-rate thugs swagger off. I smiled. Maybe Gangly got game, but Gecko got clue.

Someone was turning up the heat—someone who didn't want me sniffing around Ben Dova. And that made Ben my Suspect Numero Uno.

Would I keep on sniffing?

Indeed I would. Just as soon as I got out of the trash can.

8

Little Boys' Blew

I couldn't tell you what we studied that morning. Math didn't add up to much. Poetry lacked rhyme or reason.

All through Mr. Ratnose's class, something kept tickling the edges of my mind, like a good-night kiss from a porcupine. I couldn't quite put my finger on it, but for some reason, bullies and threats were popping up all over.

Something was afoot at Emerson Hicky Elementary.

And that foot was stinky.

Recess came, sweeter than a honey-covered fruit fly after a plateful of brussels sprouts. Hoofing it out the door, I scooted over to Natalie's room.

Her classmates were just leaving. My partner joined me.

"Heya, Chet," she said. "I've got a new one for you."

"A lead? I can't wait."

"What do you get when you pour boiling water down a rabbit hole?"

I held up a hand. "Don't tell me."

"Hot cross bunnies." She giggled.

"I asked you not to tell me. Hey, I've got one for you, too."

As we cruised up the hall, I tipped her to my run-in with the two rats.

"I hate to say I told you so," I said. "No, wait, I don't. I told you so."

"Ha, ha," said Natalie. "So, Ben's our guy?"

"Looks like. All we've gotta do is prove it."

It seemed like Viola Fuss's speech might offer the chance to gather that proof. Natalie and I turned our toes toward the grassy patch near the library, where the sandpiper's rally was about to start.

We had to duck under four kids who were hanging by their tails from an overhead beam. No, they weren't bats; they'd been strung up by Herman the Gila Monster and Erik Nidd, who were snickering and chanting, "Turn that frown upside down."

Say what you will about our bullies; they are creative.

Kids were gathering on the grass. Our client's crew, wearing VOTE FOR VIOLA! tags, herded the group into a rough kind of order.

"Let's split up," I said to Natalie. "Keep your eyes peeled for Ben or a couple of rats in shades."

"Okey-dokey, artichokey," said Natalie.

She hung out at the back of the small group. I stood near the front, by the bathrooms.

In another minute, Viola motored out of the building's shade. Eyes darting right and left, the sandpiper hopped onto a box and raised her wings.

"Fellow ... er, students," said Viola. "Ours is a ... er, wonderful school. Great teachers, great students. But we can do even better."

I won't bore you with the rest. Once was enough. But I will say this: Viola seemed to believe what she was saying. As she spoke, her nervousness faded. And kids listened.

The group looked peaceful. No Ben, no rats.

Viola's speech rambled on. Hard as it is to believe, I must have drowsed for a minute. Nearby movement snapped me back to attention.

Ben Dova strolled past the boys' bathroom. From the crowd, Rocky Rhode waved at him, but the wolverine either didn't see her or pretended not to.

Something was cooking.

Hot dang. I eased closer to the sandpiper.

Viola was saying, "And that this school *of* the

students, *by* the students, and *for* the students will become a shining—"

Ba-ka-DOOOM!

An explosion rocked the crowd!

Smoke billowed from the bathroom, followed quickly by a geyser of yellow-brown water.

I was standing right in its path.

SPLIZOOSH!

The spout pummeled me, driving me back. Viola tumbled off her box. Kids scattered.

A second later, the stench hit us.

"Eeew!" burst from a dozen throats.

Apparently, my fellow boys hadn't learned nurse Marge Supial's Bathroom Health Rule #1: Flush first, ask questions later.

Soon, the waters subsided to a steady flow.

Ears still buzzing from the blast, I wrung out my soggy coat. This would not go down as Chet Gecko's spiffiest day.

Students shook water from feathers, clothes, fur, and scales. Viola hopped to her feet, wild-eyed.

"I knew it!" she cried. "They're out to get me!" And off she skittered as fast as her shish-kebab legs could carry her.

Natalie hopped gingerly over the wet grass. She stopped a few feet away.

"Where's Ben?" I asked.

"Was he here?" she said.

"Yup. Rocky, too—just before things went ka-blooey."

"Coincidence?"

I flung droplets from my hat. "Private eyes don't believe in coincidence."

"So, what's up, buttercup?" said Natalie.

"Chew on this: Rocky and Ben are both bullies."

"Duh."

"Could they be working together to scare off Viola?"

"Why don't we go ask Rocky?" she said.

We turned to leave, but were stopped cold by a massive figure.

"Just a minute, Gecko."

I stepped back.

It was Principal Zero. A big tomcat with a bad attitude, Mr. Zero struck fear into first graders, terror into third graders, and the rest of us—he just plumb scared.

"Toilets explode, and I find you on the scene," he said. "Interesting."

"Interesting?" I said. "Nah. Meeting the winner of the annual Scarf 'n' Barf Contest—now, *that's* interesting."

"Cute." (The way he pronounced it, *cute* sounded like *extremely dumb*.) Mr. Zero's claws flashed, then retracted. "Gecko, I'm investigating this vandalism. And if I learn you had anything to do with it, you will wish you'd never been hatched. Am I clear?"

"As the windows in a Windex factory."

He growled.

"Yes, sir," I said.

"Now, scat," he said.

What can you do when the cat says scat? We scatted.

9

Green Legs and Lam

Unfortunately for our case, Natalie and I didn't have time to grill Rocky Rhode and Ben Dova before class. And I couldn't haul them before Principal Zero without proof.

So I washed off, changed my stinky T-shirt, and that was that.

Lessons passed, as lessons will (slowly and excruciatingly). When lunchtime arrived, I was primed for action. I zipped out the door with a glide in my stride.

Extortionists beware—Chet Gecko is on the prowl!

This euphoria lasted all the way down the corridor, where I bumped into Ms. Glick, the Beast of Room 3.

"Going somewhere?" she snarled.

"Uh . . . lunch?" I said.

Ms. Glick planted her scaly legs. "Have you forgotten our appointment?"

"Absolutely not." (Actually, I had.) I smiled winningly. "Just grabbing a bite before detention."

The alligator grinned back. "Don't bother. It's catered."

Rats.

Outgunned and outmaneuvered, I slouched down the hall with my captor. We passed Natalie on the way. My eyes sent her a silent message: *Help!*

No use. A minute later, the booger green door of Room 3 shut behind me. I was stuck in the slammer without bail—serving time while hoodlums ran free.

Grumbling, I slumped into a pink plastic seat. At least we would eat. My stomach rumbled like thunderstorms on Mars.

Foomp!

A tray landed on my desk. I stared. Cauliflower, beets, and lima beans?

"Where are the bugs?" I said. "I need my protein."

Ms. Glick snapped, "It's the health plate. You're on a diet."

The hefty alligator waddled to her desk and tucked into a platter laden with everything my lunch lacked.

A hubbub of distant voices reached my ears. Kids were outside having fun—other kids.

Life was most definitely not fair.

While eating, I scanned the room. Three fellow prisoners—a mouse, a pigeon, and a skink—and none of them had anything to do with my case.

I sighed.

Then the intercom squawked.

"Calling all teachers, all teachers," croaked our school secretary, Mrs. Crow. "Report to the office on the double."

Ms. Glick looked from the speaker to the four of us. She hesitated.

The box crackled again. "Come on, Glick, move your tail!"

Our warden frowned at the intercom. She growled at us, "Don't even dream about leaving this room." Then she hustled out the door.

The skink raced to the window to watch Ms. Glick pass. Seconds later, he turned back to the room. "She's gone."

We four inmates looked at one another.

"That's it," I said. "I'm buzzing this beehive."

A logjam formed at the door when we all tried to leave at once. But we squeezed into the hall. The other kids hightailed it.

Torn between getting more food and investigating, I paused. Then I beat feet toward the playground.

Cauliflower would have to hold me until I could con a late lunch from the cafeteria workers.

I scooted past an intersection.

"And where do you think you're going?" barked the voice of Ms. Glick.

Shock froze me. "I . . . was, um . . . looking for you, and—"

I turned. Natalie Attired leaned against the wall, grooming her feathers.

"You found me," she said.

"Funny, birdie. But I liked your Mrs. Crow imitation even better."

She shrugged. "The first part was the real Mrs. Crow," she said. "I just tacked on that 'move your tail' bit for chuckles."

"What's going on at the office?"

"Who cares? Ready to do some sleuthing?"

Natalie and I hustled to the playground, eyes peeled. But before we could pin down Ben or Rocky, Fate threw us a curveball.

Just past the krangleberry trees, a pinched voice hissed, "Chet Gecko!"

Since it was coming from the shrubbery, I guessed it might belong to . . .

"Viola Fuss?" I said.

"It's me," she said.

I never get tired of being right.

"Come out, Viola," said Natalie. "We've got an update on your case."

"It doesn't matter," said the sandpiper's voice from behind the trees.

Not quite the eager reception I'd expected.

"Sure it does," I said. "We're closing in on the culprit, so you'll be free to go out there and win the race."

"No, I won't," said our client.

"Why not?"

"Because," said Viola, "I just quit."

10

Bare and Square

The world took a corkscrew spin, like a lop-sided merry-go-round. I couldn't believe my ears. (Or the holes in my head, which is what we geckos have for ears.)

"What do you mean, you quit?" I said. "We're going to prove Ben threatened you, so we can get these punks off your back."

"You don't understand," Viola said. "I've gotten too much off my back already."

Natalie and I exchanged a puzzled glance.

"Stop the riddles," she said, "and come on out of the trees."

"I'm afraid you'll have to come in," said the sandpiper.

I parted the low-hanging branches, and Natalie

and I slipped between them. What I saw made my jaw drop faster than a kingfisher into a sushi bar.

"Viola?!" said Natalie.

"What happened?" I asked.

Viola Fuss looked less like a sandpiper and more like a cross between a pipe cleaner and a plucked goose. She had, in fact, been plucked. All her feathers were gone; only goose bumps (sandpiper bumps?) covered her body.

Viola tried to hide behind her spindly wings. "*This* is what happened," she said. "This is what I get for trusting you to solve my case in time."

"But who?" I said. "How?"

"And *ow!*" said Natalie with a sympathetic wince.

"They jumped me just behind the cafeteria," said the sandpiper. "All I saw was a furry paw pulling a sack over my head."

"Furry paw?" I repeated. "Ben."

Viola shivered. "Then they carried me off somewhere and . . . and . . . plucked all my beautiful feathers."

This didn't seem like the best time to ask for our fee.

"What did they say?" asked Natalie.

"That I would pay for my stubbornness. And that a stupid bird would never be president."

"Did you recognize Ben's voice?" I asked. "Or anybody's?"

Viola sniffed. "No. They left me with the sack over my head and said to count to one hundred before removing it, or I'd *really* be in trouble."

"What then?" asked Natalie.

"I went to Cool Beans and told him I quit," squeaked Viola. "Then I ran all the way here, with everyone laughing and pointing."

Natalie patted her shoulder.

"I'm ruined," she sobbed. "Father said politics was a dirty business. If only I'd listened..."

The sandpiper's words faded in my ears. My jaw clenched and my tail curled. The bad guys had been pulling the strings, making us dance.

But I was done with dancing. I wanted the dish that is best served cold (with a side of june bugs in cream sauce).

I wanted revenge.

"Natalie," I said, "you take our client—"

"*Ex*-client," said Viola.

"—to the nurse's office." I plucked some leafy branches. "Cover her up."

Natalie took the foliage. "Where are you going?"

"Me? To see a possum about a race."

The library at lunch is a lonely place. Ours smelled of ink, moldy books, triple-strength espresso, and a kindergartner who'd gotten a bit too scared during spooky story time and gone *wee, wee, wee all the way home*—if you know what I mean.

I stopped just inside the heavy oak doors and surveyed the room. A few kids picked through the bookshelves.

But the librarian was nowhere to be seen.

I headed back to his desk. "Cool Beans?" I called softly.

No answer.

The passage behind the desk bore a sign above it: RESTRICTED. STAFF ONLY.

That had never stopped me before.

Three doors lined the short hallway. Two were closed; one was ajar. (Although how a *door* can be a *jar* is one of the eternal mysteries of English.)

I eased up to it. Voices murmured indistinctly.

Through the crack, I glimpsed a hairy back and a table corner.

"Anything interesting?" a deep voice rumbled.

I whirled. Before me stood a possum as wide and tall as King Kong's refrigerator, sporting a blue beret and wraparound shades.

He was cooler than a refrigerator, too. He was Cool Beans, the librarian.

"Cool Beans," I said. "It's you."

"Last time I checked." He nodded at the room

I'd been eavesdropping on. "Wanna hook up with my latest book club?"

I shook my head. "Snooping again. I was actually looking for you."

"Just catching a quick nod," said Cool Beans. "C'mon, let's go flap our jaws."

He turned and led the way back to his desk. (Actually, *I* ended up leading the way. Possums move slower than the last day of school at the North Pole.)

"So, what's the action, Jackson?" The librarian lowered his bulk into the chair, which squeaked in protest.

I began pacing. "It's like this," I said. "My client just dropped out of the race for president."

"Viola? Man, that bird was full-out frantic when I saw her—peeled like a grape, and no mistake."

"And I don't wanna let those bird pluckers get away with it. Natalie and I suspect Ben Dova and maybe Rocky Rhode."

"Ben?" said Cool Beans. "Word from the bird is he's one rude dude."

"I need—"

Just then, a younger possum poked his nose through the hallway door.

"Uncle C," he said, "can we—hey, who's the dweeb?"

I bristled. You couldn't see much of the kid, but what I saw I didn't like.

"Chet Gecko, PI," said Cool Beans. "Chet, my nephew, Bubba Ganoosh. Bubba's crashin' with me till he straightens out and flies right."

"Aw, Uncle C, why'd you have to tell the dweeb?"

Cool Beans leveled a frosty gaze at Bubba. "What's up?"

"Oh, uh, can my book club meet after school tomorrow?"

"All reet by me," said the librarian. "You got the key."

The punk possum withdrew.

"His book club?" I said.

"Keeps him off the streets. Anywho, what jazz were we blowin'?"

"This case is kicking my keister," I said, "and the election's tomorrow. I need a quick way to flush out Ben or whoever plucked Viola."

The librarian smiled slowly (the way he did everything). "Well, bop my skull bone and call me a conga drum. I just had a brainstorm."

"Spill," I said.

"These cats were wiggin' 'cause Viola was running for prez, yes?"

"Yeah..."

"So it stands to reason, if you wanna bring 'em into the open, you oughta..."

In a flash, I saw it. "Run for president myself?"

"Exactomundo," said Cool Beans.

My mouth fell open at the simple beauty of it.

"Cool Beans," I said, "you're a possum genius."

"I hate to brag," he said. "But when a gecko's right, he's right."

11

Campaign and Caviar

As it turned out, running for student council president was so easy, even a moron could've done it. (And many have.)

With Cool Beans's help, I filled out a form and snagged a petition. All I needed were ten students' signatures, and I'd be in the race.

I scored seven of them on the soccer field. It was a snap. I just promised the kids whatever they wanted most.

Then, my salamander buddy Bo Newt staggered up, dripping water.

"Ah, just the bozo I was looking for," I said.

Bo stumbled and fell toward me. I caught his shoulders, and then I caught his scent: *Eau de Bus Station Bathroom*.

"Whew!" I winced. "What happened to you?"

He coughed and collapsed on the grass. "These three squirrels," he said. "They cornered me in the bathroom—pushing and making rude cracks about reptiles. So I started giving 'em some back."

"But *you're* an amphibian," I said.

"Oh, yeah," said Bo. "I forgot."

I indicated his drenched body. "So what'd they do?"

"Flushed me down the toilet," he said.

"Eew." I stepped back.

Bo pointed to the parking lot. "I came up through the manhole over there."

I shook my head. "I've heard of being flushed with victory, but this is ridiculous. Who were the squirrels?"

"Dunno," said the salamander. "But they kept talking about *hug* or *glug* or something."

"Well, which was it?"

Bo frowned. "Couldn't tell. Kinda hard to hear over the flushing."

With that, the class bell *clang-a-lang*ed. Lunchtime was history.

I suddenly recalled my mission. "Hey, Bo, sign this?"

My classmate scrawled his name. "What is it?" he asked.

"I'm running for president," I said. "If I win, I'll take care of those bullies."

"Gee, thanks, Chet."

"Don't mention it. Now would you do me a favor?"

"You got it."

"Hit the showers before coming back to class." I fanned the air. "Nothing personal, ace, but you stink."

Class was the usual bundle of laughs. But when recess rolled around, I perked up. Like the after-effects of a fire-ant bran muffin, things were heating up.

It was a breeze getting my ninth autograph. Shirley Chameleon has always had a crush on me, so I used that to get her to sign on the dotted line.

Shameless, I know. I blame politics.

Natalie provided the last signature. As we marched to the office to hand the petition to Principal Zero, I filled her in on my scheme.

"What do you think?" I asked.

"Well, it's simple, like my uncle Brad. But unlike Brad, it just might work."

"So you're in?"

"*In?*" she said. "I'm your new campaign manager."

Mr. Zero wasn't quite so keen. "It's the day before the election," he said.

"We've got the signatures," I said. "Cool Beans says that's all we need."

"But *you*?" he snarled, digging his claws into his wide black desk. "In student government? What's the catch?"

"No catch," I said.

"Or maybe one," said Natalie. "He caught some of the ol' school spirit!"

The tomcat looked from one of us to the other. "Uh-huh," he said.

"What's wrong, boss man?" I said.

"Gecko, the school rules say I have to let you run. But they don't say I have to like it. I think you're up to something."

I gave him my poker face. "I wonder if I know what you mean?"

"I wonder if you wonder."

We made tracks before Mr. Zero could grill me further. When your principal can literally sniff out a lie, you keep the chat to a minimum.

"So how do we spread the word that I'm running?" I asked Natalie.

"Leave that to me," she said. We hit the playground.

"Ah-*OOOO*-GAH!" bellowed Natalie, sounding exactly like an obnoxious car horn. Heads turned.

Those mockingbirds sure can mock.

"Attention, students!" cried Natalie. "You've heard the best, now try the rest. Chet Gecko for president!"

Kids gathered around. Of course, they would have assembled for a train wreck, or a four-alarm fire, or any break in their routines.

"What do you have in mind?" I muttered.

"Trust me," Natalie whispered back.

She cupped her wings around her beak and shouted, "Come one, come all, for a thrilling speech. Ladies and germs, please welcome . . . Chet Gecko!"

"A *speech*?!" I hissed at her. "What will I—"

Natalie made a grand bow and backed away.

Two or three kids clapped halfheartedly. The rest waited to see someone embarrass himself. They wouldn't have long to wait.

I hate public speaking.

"Uh . . . hey, Emerson Hicky-ites," I began. "I'm, uh, Chet Gecko . . . and, uh . . ."

"We know who ya are," shouted a burly mole, "Cheap Geek-o!"

His friends chuckled.

Sweat trickled down my face. "I'm, uh . . . running for president," I said.

"No duh!" someone else yelled.

The crowd laughed.

"Come *on*!" Natalie whispered.

The kids were getting restless. It was now or never.

"Okay," I said. "Though my name is Chet, let me be frank. Sometimes, school munches the big muffin. Schoolwork can be cheesy and greasy as an inchworm enchilada. True?"

Some kids nodded. "Yeah," said a seagull. "So?"

I waved my hands. "So if I'm elected president, I'll do something about it. No more boring subjects. History, gone! Math, gone!"

The students cheered.

"But I like math," whined a ferret. Her neighbors shushed her.

"We'll get back to the basics," I said, "like comic book reading, and ultimate Frisbee, and bungee jumping."

"Yeah!" shouted Bo Newt from the back of the mob.

I was on a roll, pumping my fist in the air. "All recesses will last an hour, and the fountains will run with soda and chocolate milk. Pizza day, every day!"

Several lizards up front started chanting, "Ge-cko, Ge-cko!"

My plan was working. A rush of power swept through me. So this was what the politics racket was all about.

I smiled and raised my arms. Victory was in the air.

Just then, a wedge of furry bodies came slamming into the crowd, and everything went to heck in a handbasket.

12

Bright Fights, Big Kitty

The playground erupted into a melee of shoving, shouting, and screaming. Fur and feathers flew. Kids tussled like the final round of a grudge match between Baker the Undertaker and Antone "The Stone" Jones.

The mob jostled me this way and that. Miss Flappy swooped past, onto a third-grade skink. Then, from out of the brawl, a black-and-tan shape plowed toward me like a spiteful torpedo.

It was Ben Dova the wolverine—rude and ripe and ready to rumble.

He pushed past Dum-Dum, who was wrestling an iguana. "Drop out of the race, bright boy," said Ben. "Or I'm gonna drop you."

"And did you make Viola drop out, too?"

The wolverine frowned. "Don't change the subject. Stop running for president—that's what I want."

"Bucko, there are two kinds of people in this world," I said, circling. "Those who care and those who don't. Me? I don't care."

He swung a massive paw. It wasn't witty repartee, but I got his point.

I ducked.

"What's the matter?" I said. "Don't trust the voters to pick you over me?"

"Whaddaya mean?" he said. "I dropped out today."

My mouth fell open. "You *what*?"

He drew himself up proudly. "I'm givin' my votes to Perry Winkel."

"Then what's it to you whether I'm president of Emerson Hicky or Queen of the Arkansas Avocado Festival?"

The wolverine lunged. I jumped back.

"You're a filthy lizard—not fit to lead." Ben edged closer.

"Says who?" I asked.

"Says Glog," he growled, feinting at my head.

I ducked again.

But the wolverine anticipated my move. His other paw swooped in and grabbed my throat, lifting me high into the air.

Natalie's face popped up over Ben's shoulder. "Chet, what can I do?"

"*Groak!*" I croaked.

"Yes, I know he's choking you, but what do you want me to do?"

I pried at my attacker's fingers, but I might as well have been trying to bend iron bars. My face turned redder than a bullfighter's undies.

"*Dnff traktn,*" I grunted.

"The tractor?" Natalie guessed. "Bring a tractor?"

I rolled my eyes and pointed my free hand at the wolverine.

"Never mind," said Natalie. "I'll think of something." She flapped off.

My eyes were beginning to bug out of my skull. My head felt like twenty pounds of concrete packed into a five-pound bag.

Suddenly—*FWEET-FWEEET!*—a piercing whistle cut through the hubbub.

"Everybody freeze!" bellowed Principal Zero's unmistakable voice.

The wolverine dropped me like a girlfriend with bad breath. He slipped into the knot of confused kids, who were looking around for the principal.

Shakily, I got to my feet and scanned the area, but I couldn't spot him.

Natalie appeared beside me. "Okey-dokey," she

said. "Now, what did you learn from your wolverine playmate?"

"Glog," I said, rubbing my throat.

"You can stop choking," said Natalie. "He's gone."

"No, birdbrain, Glog is what I learned. He said Glog thinks lizards shouldn't lead."

"Glog? Sounds like a Swedish mouthwash."

"Whoever or whatever, Glog is serious," I said. "And he's giving Ben orders. That mook has dropped out of the race, but he's still trying to make me quit."

"Call me crazy, but I get the feeling that Ben doesn't like you."

"Okay, you're crazy." Once more, I surveyed the milling crowd. "Hey, where's Mr. Zero, anyway?"

"Right here, Gecko," purred Natalie, in a dead-on impersonation of our principal.

"You," I said. "You're good."

"Marvelous impression, Miss Attired," said Mr. Zero's voice again.

I goggled. "And that time, I didn't even see your mouth move."

Natalie stared, big-eyed, at a spot over my shoulder. "It didn't," she said.

I turned.

The real Principal Zero stood behind me, smelling of tuna fish and kitty litter and trouble. "Well, well,"

he growled. "There's a rumble in the schoolyard, and here you are. Is this your handiwork?"

"Me?" I said. "I was just giving a speech, when—"

"I thought so," said Mr. Zero. "Detention for you, Chet Gecko."

"But—" I said.

"But what?" snarled the principal, with an extra-strength glare.

"Uh, he's already had detention today," said Natalie.

"Why doesn't that surprise me?" Principal Zero smoothed his whiskers. "Very well. I don't wish to seem unfair..."

"Thanks, Mr. Zero," I said.

"...so I'll make *this* detention for tomorrow," said the cat. "Get back to class." He waded into the mob, dispensing punishment.

"But recess isn't over yet," I called after him.

The class bell jangled. Recess was over.

"It's spooky how he does that," said Natalie.

13

Taking the Bully by the Horns

When a case heats up, it helps to stop, take a step back, and look at all the facts. And it really helps if you've got a brainy partner to do this with.

After school ended, Natalie and I put our gray matter to work.

"So, what have we got?" I said, as we cruised down the halls.

"Aside from your epic string of detentions?" said Natalie. "This: Somebody—maybe Perry, maybe Rocky, maybe Glog—is trying to control the election."

I shot out my tongue and nabbed a slow horsefly. Afternoon snack.

"Also, we've got, *mmf,* lots of action from the bullies," I said, chewing.

"Think they're cooking up a plan?"

I burped. "I'd be surprised to find that they could even cook."

"Still," said Natalie, "I get the feeling that some organized group is at work, dedicated to making our lives miserable."

"Teachers?"

"No, bug-brain. Some other group."

We were just passing the bike racks, a favorite after-school ambush spot for thugs. And there was Rocky Rhode, up to her old tricks—dangling a second grader over a trash can until he coughed up his money.

"Who *enjoys* making everybody's life miserable?" I said, nodding at Rocky.

"Who indeed," said Natalie. "But how do we get her to confess?"

Rocky counted the kid's change and sent the tyke off with a gentle punt.

"Well," I said, "we could just ask."

And armed only with that brilliant plan, we started toward Rocky Rhode.

Her shoulders were broad enough for a linebacker—if that linebacker had full-body spikes, too much eye makeup, and a fierce crush on Albert Einstein (don't ask). She greeted us with charm and grace.

"Shove off, screwballs!" said Rocky.

"Nice to see you, too," I said, stopping just out of reach. "It's been too long."

The horned toad snarled. "Are you cruisin' for a bruisin'?"

"No," said Natalie, "but we'd hoedown for the lowdown."

"Huh?"

We were moving too fast for her. "We likee information," I said. "You havee. Savvy?"

Rocky growled.

Natalie and I stepped back.

"You want the scoop, peeper? It's gonna cost you," said the bully.

I dug in my pocket. "What will a quarter buy us?"

"Diddly and squat," said Rocky. She circled toward us.

We circled back away.

"If you peepers got no cash, you gotta pay me another way," said the horned toad.

"What's on your mind?" I said. "If we can call it that."

"For every question I answer, we play Flinch."

"Ooh, I love games," said Natalie. "What's Flinch?"

Rocky grinned like a barracuda in the dentist's chair. "If I make you flinch, I get to pound your shoulder."

"Sure you wouldn't rather play Go Fish?" I asked.

"Flinch or nothing."

Natalie and I traded a glance. "Sounds like *your* game," she said.

"Thanks a bunch." I stopped. "But how do we know she'll tell the truth?"

Rocky Rhode loomed before me. Up close, she was a lot bigger. (And a lot funkier. These hoodlums never heard of deodorant?)

"I may be a cheat and a bully . . . ," she began.

"No," said Natalie, "you *are* a cheat and a bully."

"Oh, right," said the horned toad. "But I'm not a liar. Ask away."

"Um, here goes," I said. "Did you and Ben force Viola to quit the race?"

"First answer: nope," said Rocky. "Ben and me don't hang out anymore. He's changed."

In a lightning move, she drove her fist at my face.

"Aaugh!" I jumped back.

"Flinch!" bellowed the horned toad. She grabbed my arm and gave my shoulder a tremendous wallop.

"Ow! What was that?"

"Second answer," said Rocky. "That was Flinch."

"Wait, that wasn't a real quest—"

I shrank from her swing. Again she hammered my shoulder.

"Owie-ow-ow! That *hurt!"*

"Hee, hee," Rocky chuckled. "Next question."

Gritting my teeth, I tried for calm. My shoulder could take only so much.

"Are you in cahoots with someone called Glog?"

"Never heard of 'im," said Rocky. She feinted at my eyes with spiky fingers.

I tried my best to keep my eyes open. Naturally, I blinked.

"Flinch!"

This time, she popped me so hard, my hat came off, and my upper arm turned to jelly.

One last question. Then, a well-earned trip to the hospital.

"Rocky," I said. "You bullies have been acting really screwy lately. If you're not fixing elections, what are you up to?"

She smiled. "We're forming a union. See, I thought we'd be much more efficient if we organized. It's working out great."

"Good thinking," said Natalie.

I stared at her.

She lifted a shoulder. "What? It's clever."

Rocky kicked off another round of Flinch, with the expected results.

My whole arm throbbed. I gave a grim smile. Maybe the horned toad wasn't behind my ex-client's troubles, but I didn't want to leave her with the upper hand.

"A final question, Rocky."

She grinned wickedly and formed a fist. "Shoot."

"What is the square root of an isosceles triangle?"

Rocky blinked. "Huh?"

"Well, if you can't answer my question, I guess *I* get to play . . ."

I threw a fake punch at Rocky's horned mug. She winced in surprise.

"Flinch!" I cried, and belted her shoulder with all my might.

I hadn't counted on her spikes.

"*Yow!* Oh man!" My hand stung like a bucketful of jellyfish.

As I stumbled off with Natalie, Rocky called after us. "Hey, come back anytime. I could play Flinch all day!"

Natalie walked me home. My arm dangled like an elephant's earlobe.

"No wonder the bullies have been so busy," I said.

"Guess Rocky's not behind the threatening notes," said Natalie.

"Guess not," I said. "But at least we learned one thing."

"What's that?"

"Next time someone wants to play Flinch, *you're* asking the questions."

14

Vote Like a Butterfly, Sting Like a Flea

Election day morning felt like any other morning—a rotten way to start the day. Honestly, if the world got going at noon, I'd be a much happier gecko.

At school, election-day fever gripped the campus. Kids waved flags, chewed Perry 4 Prez gum, and lined up at the library to cast their votes.

I had no illusions. Perry would easily beat Popper and me. But I didn't much care about my political career.

What bothered me was, my unseen foe was still one step ahead—making Viola quit, Ben attack me, and pulling who knows what other dirty tricks?

And if I didn't catch up with him, her, or them today, that was it.

Game over.

Natalie and I met at recess in the voting line, which snaked out the library door and onto the grass.

"So," I said, "it's not Ben, since he's dropped out. And it's not Rocky . . ."

"Who does that leave?" she said. "Perry Winkel, or this Glog guy?"

"Must be," I said. We shuffled with the line, up onto the library steps.

Natalie cocked her head. "But something doesn't make sense. With Viola gone, Perry's gonna win by a landslide. Why would he or his goons feel threatened by you?"

"Because of my winning personality?"

"Oh, sure." She smirked. "You'll probably capture the smart-aleck vote."

"Don't underestimate my people," I said. "We're small but mighty."

Natalie and I entered the library. As we waited, Popper passed us coming out. She *boing*ed up like a pogo stick doing hip-hop.

"Hey, hi, hi, you guys!" she said. "Going to vote?"

"Nah," I said, "we heard they were passing out free earwig fudge bars."

For a moment, she frowned in confusion, then brightened. "Well, enjoy! This was a fun, fun race. And may the best inny-unny-animal win!"

I watched her go. "It's candidates like her who give politics a bad name."

We cast our votes with the rest of the kids, and then pushed out the doors.

"Who'd you vote for?" I asked Natalie.

"My lips are sealed," she said.

I raised an eyebrow. "Birds don't have lips."

"Nevertheless."

We were at loose ends. To stop the plot, we had to prove Perry or Glog was breaking the rules—and do it before the votes were tallied. Cool Beans would count the ballots that evening, long after school was out.

We had less than four hours—minus my lunchtime detention.

"Let's split up," I said. "I'll try to find Glog; you go shadow Perry."

"I think he's already got a shadow," said Natalie.

I rolled my eyes. "Just stick with him."

"Forsooth, great sleuth!"

I shot her a look.

"What," she said, "you don't like Shakespeare?"

Recess disappeared like a snow cone dropped on a summer sidewalk. I asked kids about Glog, but all I got were odd looks, a few *buzz offs*, and an invitation to a Norwegian fish-slapping dance.

Come class time, I was none the wiser. That condition lasted throughout my morning lessons—despite Mr. Ratnose's best efforts.

I sulked through the long minutes. It wasn't fair that I got two days of detention just for being in the wrong place at the wrong time.

Yeah, I know. Tough-guy private eyes don't sulk. But let's see Sherlock Holmes or Sam Spade face my frustrations and come up smiling.

By the time lunch arrived, my mood was as foul as a spoiled stinkbug casserole. I dragged my tail out the door of Mr. Ratnose's classroom and down the hall.

At the intersection, I paused. One corridor led to detention; one led to freedom.

Which would I pick?

"Chet Gecko!" yelled the grumpy gator Ms. Glick from outside Room 3. "Get your scaly tail over here."

Detention it was.

Then I slouched into Room 3, and strangely enough, things looked sunnier. Ben Dova and Dum-Dum the badger sat moping by the windows. (They'd been so palsy-walsy lately, they even sulked together.)

"Hiya, girls," I said. "Whatcha in for?"

"Somebody ratted us out for breaking up your speech," wheezed Dum-Dum in his odd, high voice.

"Well, well," I said. "Small world, isn't it?"

"Not as small as your pea-brain," snarled Ben. They chuckled.

Before I could punish them with my wit, a heavy hand clamped onto my shoulder.

"Park your carcass," said Ms. Glick. "And zip your lip. You're not going anywhere this time." She passed out our lunches, and then chained and pad-locked the door.

I sat in the next row over from the two cutie-pies, far enough to be out of reach, but close enough to eavesdrop. As I munched, I kept my ears tuned to Ben and Dum-Dum, but they behaved like model prisoners.

I waited until Ms. Glick was busy disciplining a surly rodent up front. "What's the matter?" I whispered to Ben. "Did Glog desert you?"

He stared with hooded eyes. "Never," he said.

"Who is Glog, anyway? A sixth grader? A teacher?"

Ben and Dum-Dum chuckled. "You don't know squat about Glog," said Ben.

"Oh, yeah?" I taunted. "Show me how dumb I am."

But Ms. Glick shushed us, and I resumed chewing my tasteless food.

A flicker of movement caught my eye. Someone was skulking outside the open window, beyond Ms.

Glick's line of sight: a sneaky-looking weasel in dark glasses and a fluorescent orange tank top. Spy-Girl Barbie.

I felt I'd seen her before, but couldn't place her.

Spy-Girl waved at the two brutes. As Ben and Dum-Dum watched, the weasel folded a note into a paper airplane and lofted it through the window.

Her aim was as bad as her fashion sense.

The plane wobbled through the air, past Dum-Dum's grasp, and headed straight for me. Just at that moment, Ms. Glick chose to look up.

I shot out my tongue and snagged the missile— *glomph!*

"What's going on there?" snarled the Beast of Room 3. The weasel pulled a vanishing act.

"Um, wreally bwig cwockroach," I mumbled around the message.

The wolverine and badger stared daggers at me. If we'd been a knife-throwing act, they'd have carved me into flank steaks in no time flat.

"Dova, Dumbrowski—eyes front!" Ms. Glick harrumphed. "And Gecko, no snacking during detention." She returned to grading tests.

When the coast was clear, I fished the soggy note from my mouth.

Yuck. I hate it when girls write on perfumed paper.

The message read:

URRGENT—
GLOGG AT BOOK KLUB. MEET TODDAY
AT 3:30.

LUV,
CYDNI

Something struck me as familiar about the crummy handwriting and worse spelling. *Hmm.*

I glanced over at the wolverine and badger. These bruisers were no book club members. In fact, I'd have been willing to bet that neither one had read anything since his last report card, which mostly consisted of one letter: F.

So Glog was going to be at the book club, eh?

I didn't know exactly what this club was up to, but I did know one thing. It was about to get a new member: one Chet "Super Snooper" Gecko.

I just hoped the "book" they were reading didn't turn out to be a cliff-hanger.

15

Bubba Ganoosh

Detention didn't last any longer than the Roman Empire, the Jurassic period, or the World's Most Boring Movies marathon. It just seemed that way.

At long last, Ms. Glick unlocked the door. I scooted out before the other delinquents, making sure to give Ben and Dum-Dum the slip.

My hunch told me Glog's book club could hold the answers to all the latest strangeness at Emerson Hicky. If I could catch the phony literature lovers working their mischief, I could write a new ending to their twisted story.

During late recess, Natalie and I met by the scrofulous tree to regroup.

"I didn't learn anything from watching Perry," she said. "He campaigned, he voted, he ate lunch, and he played basketball. Bo-ring."

"Wait till you hear about *my* lunch," I said, and filled her in on the latest.

Natalie perked up. "That's what I call a lead," she said. "Hey, that spy weasel—did she look like the one we saw casing Viola's locker?"

I smacked my head. "Of course! *That's* where I've seen her before."

"Show me the message," said Natalie. I showed her.

"This looks like the writing on those mean notes Viola got," she said.

"So *that's* why it seemed so familiar."

Natalie smirked. "Lucky you've got me around to connect the dots."

"Dots what friends are for," I said. "Now, let's figure out how to bust Glog and his book club."

"If only we could bring a teacher to catch them making their mischief."

"Better yet," I said, "we'll bring the mischief-making to the teacher. Tell me, does your brother still work for the newspaper?"

After school, Natalie and I sat on the rooftop across from the library. She had borrowed her brother's tape recorder. We were loaded and ready to go.

Our goal: plant the device before the meeting began. We waited for school to empty out. Ten minutes dragged by like a caterpillar with sprained ankles.

"I hate waiting," said Natalie.

"Me, too."

A few more minutes limped along.

"I know how to pass the time," said Natalie.

"Lay it on me," I said.

"What do you get when you cross a fly with an elephant?"

I just shook my head.

"A zipper that never forgets!" Natalie squawked. "Fly . . . zipper . . . get it? Okay, how do you spot an elephant hiding in a bowl of M&M's?"

After what felt like a century later, Natalie had run through all her elephant jokes. I peeked over the roof's edge.

All clear.

School was deserted. It was as quiet as a monster movie graveyard just before the zombies come to life.

"Showtime," I said.

Natalie glided to the grass, and I slid down a pole to join her. From way down the hall came the *skritch-skritch* of the janitor's raking.

We hotfooted it over to the library.

So far, so good.

I tried the library door. Locked. And the keyhole was too small for me to pick the lock with my tail tip. *Drat.*

Natalie peered through a window. "Empty. You sure that note is for real?"

"Real as the ten pages of homework I'm avoiding right now," I said, casing the joint. "So how are these goons getting into their meeting?"

"Breaking in?" said Natalie.

"Naw...too messy. Cool Beans wouldn't stand for it. *Hmm*...Cool Beans..."

"What about him?"

A picture sprang to mind—a sneering possum telling Cool Beans about a book club meeting.

"I've got it!" I said.

"What?" said Natalie. "Parasites?"

"Not exactly. Bubba Ganoosh—Cool Beans's nephew. He has the key, and he's supervising this book club. So if we catch him first..."

"We get the key."

Natalie and I settled into the bushes on either side of the door and waited. Soon, an off-key whistling grated on our ears.

I peered between the leaves.

Bubba Ganoosh sauntered up the pathway. He wore a sneer like it was his natural expression (which, come to think of it, it probably was). The possum's fur was matted and gray, and his backward baseball cap advertised his rebel attitude.

As he approached, I realized something important: Natalie and I had no plan for neutralizing Bubba. We also had no net, no sack, no handcuffs.

That left trickery.

I stepped out from the shrubbery. "Hey, ace. Am I glad to see you!"

"You are?" Bubba frowned. "Who are you?"

"Chet Gecko," I said, "friend of your uncle's. Remember?"

Recognition dawned in his mud brown eyes. "Oh, yeah. The dweeb. What were you doing in the bushes?"

Glancing over his shoulder at Natalie, I thought fast. "Oh, uh...hiding. Yeah, see, there's this... um, psycho on the loose."

"Psycho?"

"Yeah," I said, making a shooing motion at Natalie. "He's really dangerous and uh, deranged."

Bubba eyed me. "You sure *he's* the deranged one?"

Natalie crept backward toward the edge of the library, watching us.

"Oh, uh, ha-ha," I said. I leaned closer. "Yeah, he's on the loose, alrighty, and headed this way. They say we're all supposed to hide."

"I dunno," said the possum. "Sounds like a load of horse hockey."

He started turning toward the door, with Natalie still in plain sight.

"It's true!" I grabbed his arm. "In fact, I can hear the psycho now."

Bubba cocked his head. "I don't hear nothin'."

"Yeah," I said, glaring at Natalie. "There it is again!"

She nodded and uncorked the longest, creepiest psycho laugh I'd ever heard. "Mwah-ha-ha-ha-ha-hee-*heeee*!"

The possum's eyes went wide. He whirled, looking for the source of the noise, but Natalie had slipped around the corner.

"Quick!" he hissed. "Inside!"

Bubba fumbled with the keys. A possum in panic mode still moves slower than the last minutes of a parent-teacher conference.

I glanced around, afraid that the book club members might catch us.

"Let me," I said, grabbing the keys.

Natalie cackled again, for good measure.

"Hurry!" said Bubba.

I hustled the possum indoors. "That was close!" I said. "Why don't you hide someplace safe, and I'll keep watch."

He scanned the library. "Where should I go?"

I remembered the back hall. "Isn't there a storage room that locks?"

"Good idea!" said Bubba. He scooted for it at the speed of paint drying.

I glanced at the wall clock above the ballot boxes. It was 3:25. Glog's goons could show up at any moment.

Putting a shoulder to Bubba's back, I hurried him into the storeroom.

"I'll stand guard," I said. "Whatever happens— whatever you may hear—don't budge."

"I'll play possum," said Bubba.

I locked him in. The next door in the hallway opened with a creak: the conference room. I flicked on the lights.

Where could I hide the tape recorder?

Under the table? Too risky. On the ceiling? Too exposed. I slipped the machine into a supply drawer, turned it on, and left the drawer ajar.

Now, to make my getaway . . . I stepped into the hall.

Click. The library door opened.

A sudden chatter of voices sent adrenaline sizzling through my veins like the sugar rush from a ten-foot-tall chocolate bunny.

Too late to escape.

Glog's gang was here.

16

Gopher Broke

With seconds to spare, I darted back into the meeting room, lunged for the recycling bin, and dived inside. Quietly I lowered the plastic lid.

Footsteps scuffed in the hallway.

"Didn't see him," said a sultry voice. "But I'm sure he's around."

"It doesn't matter," an oily voice replied. "He opened the door; that's his main job. The poor fool actually thinks we'll make him one of us."

"Some lead, some follow," said Sultry Voice, with a chuckle.

That voice sounded maddeningly familiar, but I couldn't place it. All I could tell was, both speakers were girls. Other footsteps and voices followed as more kids shuffled into the room.

The contents of the recycling bin pressed in on me. Papers prickled my nose. A wet soda bottle dug into my leg. A sharp object poked my back; it felt like someone was hoping to recycle a cactus.

But I couldn't budge. Any move would give me away.

"Is everyone here?" Oily Voice asked.

"Everyone except Dum-Dum and Ben," rasped a boy's voice.

"Let's begin," said Sultry Voice.

A sharp *flick,* and the perfumy smell of incense drifted on the air. A wild buzzing filled the room, like a rattlesnake taking a percussion solo. Then it died away.

"Oh, Most Secret and Powerful One, we gather in your fuzzy name," chanted Sultry Voice.

"Glog!" the group responded.

"We ask your help, to do your dread work, and purify this school."

"GLOG!" chanted the group, louder.

"Help us, guide us, stand by us as we act to make our dreams reality!"

"GLOG!" the gang roared.

"So be it, and so it be," said Sultry Voice.

I itched to burst out and confront them. (I also itched from the stupid paper tickling my nose.) But I had to wait until I got the incriminating words on tape.

A distant door banged. Heavy footsteps pounded into the room.

Was it Glog?

"Sorry I'm late," boomed a rough voice. Ben Dova.

"We wuz held up cuz the gecko stole our message," said a high, tight voice. Dum-Dum Dumbrowski?

"No matter," said Sultry Voice. "We will deal with him later. Now, how goes the takeover?"

Raspy Voice responded. "Splendidly, O Exalted One. Glog will seize power tomorrow. All that's left is to stuff those boxes."

"Are you sure we need to do that?" said Oily Voice. "With only the frog and that ridiculous gecko left in the race, our boy may have already won."

Ridiculous gecko? Ooh, I was gonna *love* busting these guys.

"You bet yer bottom boots I'm winnin'," said a corn-fried voice. Perry?

"We take no chances," said Sultry Voice. "Ben, Dum-Dum?"

"Yes, Nadia."

Nadia? I could barely restrain myself. Sultry Voice was Nadia Nyce, Perry's campaign manager? This got better and better.

"Go into the other room and bring the ballot boxes here," said Nadia.

"Will I be a member after this?" whined Ben. "You promised if I supported Perry and helped Dum-Dum and dropped out of the union—"

So *that* explained the split between Rocky and Ben.

Nadia's voice sharpened. "When our goal is won, Glog will reward those who helped gain the victory."

Ben and Dum-Dum left the room.

"Fool," said Oily Voice. The others chuckled.

"It was *so* easy to trick him into dropping out," said Nadia.

My itch was nearly unbearable. Something crawled over my feet. The sweet smoke made my nose twitch in a most alarming way. I gritted my teeth.

Just a little while longer . . .

Footsteps returned. The door closed. Several objects thumped onto the table.

"Who has the new ballots?" said Oily Voice.

"Here," said Raspy Voice. A bag rustled. "How do you—"

The world turns on *if only*s. If only Cool Beans had kept his recycling bin cleaner. If only it hadn't attracted red fire ants.

And if only one ant hadn't chosen that very moment to chomp on my tail.

Hard.

"YeeeOWWWW!" I screamed, launching up from the paper and plastics like a recycling rocket.

I landed on the cool tile floor. Around me a dozen faces gaped—Ben, Dum-Dum, Perry, Nadia, the tough-guy rats, Miss Flappy, Spy-Girl Barbie, and a mean looking assortment of weasels and badgers.

"Give up!" I cried.

My entrance had showered papers around the room and some came to rest against the incense sticks. Smoke swirled, tickling my nose worse than a dozen big brothers.

"The play-ay-ayce is surrounded," I said. "We've got you dead to ri-hi-hi-*CHOO!*-ights."

My supersonic sneeze scattered the pile of ballots on the table. Oops.

"Is that so?" said Nadia. The mink wore a goofy headdress bristling with horns, feathers, fringes, and spangles. She looked like Sitting Bull as a Las Vegas showgirl.

"I think *we've* got *you*," said Miss Flappy with a wicked grin.

I scanned the room. She was right. They did.

Where was Natalie when I needed her?

The furry gang closed in on me.

"So," I said, "which one of you is Glog?"

Chuckles all around. "Ya nitwit," sneered Burly Rat. "We're *all* Glog."

"Huh?"

A smile teased Nadia's lips. She pointed to a gopher statue with candles on its head. "The Grand and Loyal Order of the Golden Gopher. That's GLOGG, smart guy. And we're going to rid this school of your kind."

Before they grabbed me, I scanned desperately for a weak link. I found it.

"Dum-Dum!" I cried, pointing past his left shoulder. "Behind you!"

True to his name, he looked.

I darted past the badger and dived onto my belly, sliding under the table.

On the far side,
I popped up.

"So long,
suckers!" I sprang
for the exit.

The members
of GLOGG roared
in rage.

"Get him!" cried Nadia.

Gangly Rat vaulted the
table and blocked the door.

Dang!

Trapped, I leaped for
the wall. Paws clutched at
my tail, but I scrambled
upward.

Whap! A thrown book just missed my head.

I glanced down. Burly Rat hurled a coffee cup—*kahssh!*

"Tsk, tsk," I said. "Cool Beans won't like that."

"Don't let him escape!" cried Nadia.

The group fanned out across the room. I checked their number. All were mammals—not a bird or a lizard in sight. That meant no wall climbers.

"I can hang out on the ceiling all day long," I said. "Come and get me, you furballs!"

Smoke rose to meet me. Snarls and frowny faces greeted my taunt—except for one ugly face: The bat was smiling.

And then I remembered. Bats can fly.

"Foolish Gecko," she said, flexing her wings. "Say nighty-night. You're going down."

And with a flap, she launched herself straight at me.

17

Bite the Ballot

What happened next is still somewhat of a blur, like a runaway preschooler at bath time. But here's what I remember.

A deafening *BEEP-BEEP-BEEP* went off near my head, almost making me lose my grip. Hard on its heels came a *pssssh,* as a half-dozen ceiling sprinklers dumped their water all at once.

The bat caught a snootful of spray and tumbled back onto the table like a lead bumblebee.

"Aaugh!" cried the GLOGGers.

Nadia tried to shield the bogus ballots with her body, but it was too late. Streams of water soaked the pile of paper.

Boom! The door banged open.

"What in the blue blazes of bop is goin' on here?" Cool Beans demanded.

The massive possum stood with hands on hips, surveying the wreckage. Even through his shades, the librarian's eyes were shooting fire.

Natalie peered around him. "Looks like a ballot box stuffing party gone bad."

I climbed down from my perch and retrieved the damp tape recorder from its drawer. Luckily, it was still running.

"And we've got the whole thing on tape," I said.

Cool Beans took the machine. "Crazy," he said. "This recording is gonna make the top ten on Mr. Zero's Hit Parade."

I looked around at the bedraggled plotters, and I knew who'd be getting the hits. Mr. Zero does love his spanking machine.

While Cool Beans called our principal and dealt with the soggy members of GLOGG, I squelched homeward with Natalie.

"If you and Cool Beans hadn't blown in, I'd have been all washed up," I said.

"You mean, more than you already are," said Natalie.

I wrung out my sleeves. "So how'd you know to come in after me?"

"I hung around outside," she said. "And when I saw those mugs going in, I figured you were cornered."

"You don't know the half of it."

We passed through the parking lot and onto the peaceful street.

"So I found Cool Beans waiting in the teachers' lounge for his nephew to call," she said.

"Oh, yeah," I said. "Bubba."

Natalie waved a wing. "He was worried, 'cause Bubba was supposed to give him some signal that everything was okay with the book club."

"What signal?"

"He calls and lets the phone ring a couple times."

"Ah," I said. "The possum always rings twice."

"What?"

"Nothing. Go on."

"I told Cool Beans about the fake book club, and he hustled over to break it up."

Shaking water off my hat, I asked, "What took you guys so long?"

Natalie raised an eyebrow. "Ever try to hurry a possum?"

"Point taken."

We ambled up the street in silence awhile. The sun slanted through the trees.

"Hey," said Natalie. "Speaking of possums, whatever happened to Bubba?"

I gave her a half smile. "He's, uh, still playing possum."

Natalie frowned. "And when are you going to let Cool Beans know where he is?"

"All in good time, birdie. All in good time."

The next day, the GLOGG caper was big news all over school. Apparently, these goofballs had formed their secret society to establish the rule of mammals. They had scared off Viola, broken up my speech, and bombed the bathroom.

They had even thrown me off their trail by having the rats warn me away from Ben, making me think the wolverine was behind it all.

If we hadn't stopped the plotters, GLOGG would've tried to turn Emerson Hicky into a mammals-only school. Personally, I felt they deserved each other. But I had a few more years left at the dump, and I'd gotten used to it.

Natalie and I were eating sack lunches under the scrofulous tree when some other news arrived, in the shape of a yellow-and-green bouncing ball.

"Hey there, hi there, ho there!" cried Popper, all aquiver.

"Hey, peewee," I said. "What's shaking? Other than you, I mean."

"Haven't you heard?" she said.

"Heard what?" asked Natalie.

Popper's eyes grew wider than a hippo's belt. "A bunch of rotten-dirty rotten cheaters tried to get that Porry-Perry guy elected."

"We know," I said. "We stopped 'em."

"And so Mr. Zero envela...invala—uh, didn't count his vee-vi-votes!"

"What's that mean?" asked Natalie.

The little frog hooked a thumb at her chest. "I'm the new pippity-president!"

My jaw dropped open. I stared into her mile-wide grin. "You?"

"Me!"

Natalie turned to me. "I don't believe it."

"There's more, more, more!" Popper pogo-ed up and down in a blur.

"More?" I asked.

"The runnity-runner-up gets to be vice president!"

I held up a palm. "Hang on," I said. "If Viola and Ben dropped out, and Perry was disqualified, then who's left?"

"You," said Natalie.

"No way."

"Yup, yeah, uh-huh," said Popper. "You got two votes. See ya at studity-student council!" And she vibrated off.

I looked at Natalie. "Two votes, eh? Would one of those be yours?"

She whistled and stared up at the clouds. "I'll never tell."

"Birdie," I said, "here's another fine mess you've gotten me into."

Has Chet finally met his match?
Find out in
KEY LARDO

It all started with a muffin. And despite my best intentions, it went downhill from there, quicker than a walrus on roller skates.

Wednesday is Italian Day in the cafeteria. On this particular Wednesday, Mrs. Bagoong and her cooks had worked their usual magic—spaghetti with millipede meatballs, eggplant à la fungus gnat, and honeyglazed Madagascan Hissing Cockroach muffins.

The muffins set off a taste explosion that had my tongue dancing the Madagascan Mambo (or whatever kind of hoofing they do over there).

I pushed back from the table and headed over to score another one. Most kids don't get to have seconds.

But I'm not most kids.

Bellying up to the lunch counter, I could tell that the baked goodies had been a hit. All had vanished but one.

And that one had Chet Gecko's name on it.

"Hey, Brown Eyes," I said to Mrs. Bagoong. "What would it—"

A plump figure barged in front of me. "I say, dear

madam," he said. "Could a poor bloke please have another of those heavenly muffins?"

Mrs. Bagoong's smile sent dimples burrowing into her scaly face. "Why, how you talk," said the big iguana. "There's one left, just for you."

She lifted the golden muffin with her tongs.

"But!" I squawked. "That's mine!"

The queen of the lunchroom raised an eyebrow. "Now, now. This charming penguin asked first, and he asked politely."

"But—"

Mrs. Bagoong's frown could have brought on an eclipse at high noon. "Why, Chet Gecko," she said. "I'm surprised at you. Can't you be generous with the new boy?"

"New boy?"

I stepped back to size up the muffin thief.

His webbed feet were planted wide, to support his swollen belly. The penguin's broad butt tapered to a small head, giving him the look of a bowling pin that needed to hit Weight Watchers.

Topping it all off were a midnight blue bow tie and bowler that would've looked better on a banker than a school kid.

Having snagged my treat, the creature turned with a vague smile.

"Don't believe we've met," he said, extending a flipper. "The name's Bland. James Bland."

He reeked of fermented fish and onions.

My eyes watered. I returned the briefest handshake. "Gecko. Chet Gecko."

Mrs. Bagoong beamed. "So nice to see y'all getting along. James, you've found a new friend already."

"Friend?" I said. "Now, wait just—"

The lunch lady's glare cut me off like a sushi chef hacking a halibut. "Chet will be *happy* to show you around, introduce you." Her eyes completed the thought: *If he ever wants to have seconds in my lunchroom again.*

I heaved a sigh. A good detective can tell when he's outmaneuvered.

"All right, Bland. Come on."

"Good-o," said the penguin. "Ta-ta, madam!" He waved a flipper at Mrs. Bagoong, who simpered back at him. And if you don't think the sight of a simpering iguana is enough to curdle your French fries, think again.

I shuffled toward the nearest table. "So, uh, where are you from?"

"Down Under actually, but I've spent donkey's years in Albion," he said.

"Living with a donkey?"

"No, living in England."

Swell. Not only was he a muffin bandit, the guy could barely speak English.

I eyeballed his plate. "Pretty big dessert after such a full meal. Need help?"

"Oh, I'll muddle through," said James Bland. He plunged his beak into the treat and gobbled down about half of it.

So much for the old guilt trick.

A ragtag group of kids ringed the table. Among them sat Frenchy LaTrine, Bo and Tony Newt, Cassandra the Stool Pigeon, and Shirley Chameleon (who had a wicked crush on me)—all eating, laughing, and spraying food.

"Hey, sports fans," I said. "This is James Blond."

"Bland," said the penguin.

"Ain't that the truth," I said. "Anyway, he's a new kid, from Down Over."

"Under," said Bland.

"Whatever." I gestured to the group. "James, guys; guys, James."

The penguin bowed. "A pleasure to make your acquaintance," he said.

Frenchy LaTrine giggled. "Cool accent!"

"Do you know any kangaroos personally?" asked Tony Newt.

"A few," said the penguin. He scarfed down the

rest of the muffin as I watched sadly. "I say, do you know what they call a lazy kangaroo?"

"No, what?" said Frenchy.

"A pouch potato," said Bland.

The girls shrieked with laughter; even my buddy Bo chuckled.

I didn't care. So what if the new guy was funny?

Shirley Chameleon elbowed Bo Newt. "Scoot over for James."

She didn't suggest they make room for me.

The penguin squeezed his bubble butt in between them. He vacuumed the last muffin fragments off Shirley's plate.

"What do you do for *fun,* James?" she asked, batting her eyes.

I didn't care. Although Shirley had a crush on *me,* she was free to fling her cooties wherever she wanted.

Bland angled his hat. "Actually, I do a spot of detective work," he said.

Now, wait just a boll-weevil-pickin' minute.

Look for more mysteries from
the Tattered Casebook of Chet Gecko
in hardcover and paperback

Case #1 *The Chameleon Wore Chartreuse*

Some cases start rough, some cases start easy. This one started with a dame. (That's what we private eyes call a girl.) She was cute and green and scaly. She looked like trouble and smelled like ... grasshoppers.

Shirley Chameleon came to me when her little brother, Billy, turned up missing. (I suspect she also came to spread cooties, but that's another story.) She turned on the tears. She promised me some stinkbug pie. I said I'd find the brat.

But when his trail led to a certain stinky-breathed, bad-tempered, jumbo-sized Gila monster, I thought I'd bitten off more than I could chew. Worse, I had to chew fast: If I didn't find Billy in time, it would be bye-bye, stinkbug pie.

Case #2 *The Mystery of Mr. Nice*

How would you know if some criminal mastermind tried to impersonate your principal? My first clue: He was nice to me.

This fiend tried everything—flattery, friendship, food—but he still couldn't keep me off the case. Natalie and I followed a trail of clues as thin as the cheese on a cafeteria hamburger. And we found a ring of corruption that went from the janitor right up to Mr. Big.

In the nick of time, we rescued Principal Zero and busted up the PTA meeting, putting a stop to the evil genius. And what thanks did we get? Just the usual. A cold handshake and a warm soda.

But that's all in a day's work for a private eye.

Case #3 *Farewell, My Lunchbag*

If danger is my business, then dinner is my passion. I'll take any case if the pay is right. And what pay could be better than Mothloaf Surprise?

At least that's what I thought. But in this particular case, I bit off more than I could chew.

Cafeteria lady Mrs. Bagoong hired me to track down whoever was stealing her food supplies. The long, slimy trail led too close to my own backyard for comfort.

And much, much too close to the deadly Jimmy "King" Cobra. Without the help of Natalie Attired and our school janitor, Maureen DeBree, I would've been gecko sushi.

Case #4 *The Big Nap*

My grades were lower than a salamander's slippers, and my bank account was trying to crawl under a duck's belly. So why did I take a case that didn't pay anything?

Put it this way: Would *you* stand by and watch some

evil power turn *your* classmates into hypnotized zombies? (If that wasn't just what normally happened to them in math class, I mean.)

My investigations revealed a plot meaner than a roomful of rhinos with diaper rash.

Someone at Emerson Hicky was using a sinister video game to put more and more students into la-la-land. And it was up to me to stop it, pronto—before that someone caught up with me and I found myself taking the Big Nap.

Case #5 *The Hamster of the Baskervilles*

Elementary school is a wild place. But this was ridiculous.

Someone—or some*thing*—was tearing up Emerson Hicky. Classrooms were trashed. Walls were gnawed. Mysterious tunnels riddled the playground like worm chunks in a pan of earthworm lasagna.

But nobody could spot the culprit, let alone catch him.

I don't believe in the supernatural. My idea of voodoo is my mom's cockroach-ripple ice cream.

Then, a teacher reported seeing a monster on full-moon night, and I got the call.

At the end of a twisted trail of clues, I had to answer the burning question: Was it a vicious, supernatural were-hamster on the loose, or just another Science Fair project gone wrong?

Case #6 *This Gum for Hire*

Never thought I'd see the day when one of my worst enemies would hire me for a case. Herman the Gila Monster was a sixth-grade hoodlum with a first-rate left hook. He told me someone was disappearing the football team, and he had to put a stop to it. *Big whoop.*

He told me he was being blamed for the kidnappings, and he had to clear his name. *Boo hoo.*

Then he said that I could either take the case and earn a nice reward, or have my face rearranged like a bargain-basement Picasso painted by a spastic chimp.

I took the case.

But before I could find the kidnapper, I had to go undercover. And that meant facing something that scared me worse than a chorus line of criminals in steel-toed boots: P.E. class.

Case #7 *The Malted Falcon*

It was tall, dark, and chocolatey—the stuff dreams are made of. It was a treat so titanic that nobody had been able to finish one single-handedly (or even single-mouthedly). It was the Malted Falcon.

How far would you go for the ultimate dessert? Somebody went too far, and that's where I came in.

The local sweets shop held a contest. The prize: a year's supply of free Malted Falcons. Some lucky kid scored the winning ticket. She brought it to school for show-and-tell.

But after she showed it, somebody swiped it. And no one would tell where it went.

Following a strong hunch and an even stronger sweet tooth, I tracked the ticket through a web of lies more tangled than a rattlesnake doing the rumba. But the time to claim the prize was fast approaching. Would the villain get the sweet treat—or his just desserts?

Case #8 *Trouble Is My Beeswax*

Okay, I confess. When test time rolls around, I'm as tempted as the next lizard to let my eyeballs do the walking . . . to my neighbor's paper.

But Mrs. Gecko didn't raise no cheaters. (Some language manglers, perhaps.) So when a routine investigation uncovered a test-cheating ring at Emerson Hicky, I gave myself a new case: Put the cheaters out of business.

Easier said than done. Those double-dealers were slicker than a frog's fanny and twice as slimy.

Oh, and there was one other small problem: The finger of suspicion pointed to two dames. The ringleader was either the glamorous Lacey Vail, or my own classmate Shirley Chameleon.

Sheesh. The only thing I hate worse than an empty Pillbug Crunch wrapper is a case full of dizzy dames.

Case #9 *Give My Regrets to Broadway*

Some things you can't escape, however hard you try—like dentist appointments, visits with strange-smelling relatives, and being in the fourth-grade play. I had always left the acting to my smart-aleck pal, Natalie, but then one day it was my turn in the spotlight.

Stage fright? Me? You're talking about a gecko who has laughed at danger, chuckled at catastrophe, and sneezed at sinister plots.

I was terrified.

Not because of the acting, mind you. The script called for me to share a major lip-lock with Shirley Chameleon—Cootie Queen of the Universe!

And while I was trying to avoid that trap, a simple missing-persons case took a turn for the worse—right into the middle of my play. Would opening night spell curtains for my client? And, more important, would someone invent a cure for cooties? But no matter—whatever happens, the sleuth must go on.

Case #10 *Murder, My Tweet*

Some things at school you can count on. Pop quizzes always pop up just after you've spent your study time studying comics. Chef's Surprise is always a surprise, but never a good one. And no matter how much you learn today, they always make you come back tomorrow.

But sometimes, Emerson Hicky amazes you. And just like finding a killer bee in a box of Earwig Puffs, you're left shocked, stung, and discombobulated.

Foul play struck at my school; that's nothing new. But then the finger of suspicion pointed straight at my favorite fowl: Natalie Attired. Framed as a blackmailer, my partner was booted out of Emerson Hicky quicker than a hoptoad on a hot plate.

I tackled the case for free. Mess with my partner, mess with me.

Then things took a turn for the worse. Just when I thought I might clear her name, Natalie disappeared. And worse still, she left behind one clue: a reddish smear that looked kinda like the jelly from a beetle-jelly sandwich but raised an ugly question: Was it murder, or something serious?